THE PIRATE KING

KRONUS
THE
CLAWED MENACE

With special thanks to Allan Frewin Jones
For Linda Brignall, a great librarian

www.beastquest.co.uk

ORCHARD BOOKS
338 Euston Road, London NW1 3BH
Orchard Books Australia
Level 17/207 Kent St, Sydney, NSW 2000

A Paperback Original
First published in Great Britain in 2011

Beast Quest is a registered trademark of Beast Quest Limited
Series created by Working Partners Limited, London

Text © Beast Quest Limited 2011
Cover and inside illustrations by Steve Sims © Orchard Books 2011

A CIP catalogue record for this book is available from
the British Library.

ISBN 978 1 40831 314 5

Printed and bound in China by Imago

The paper and board used in this paperback are natural recyclable
products made from wood grown in sustainable forests. The
manufacturing processes conform to the environmental regulations of
the country of origin.

Orchard Books is a division of Hachette Children's Books,
an Hachette UK company

www.hachette.co.uk

KRONUS
THE
CLAWED MENACE

BY ADAM BLADE

ORCHARD BOOKS

THE

WESTERN OCEAN

THE FOREST
OF FEAR

THE W

THE RUBY DESERT

SPIN

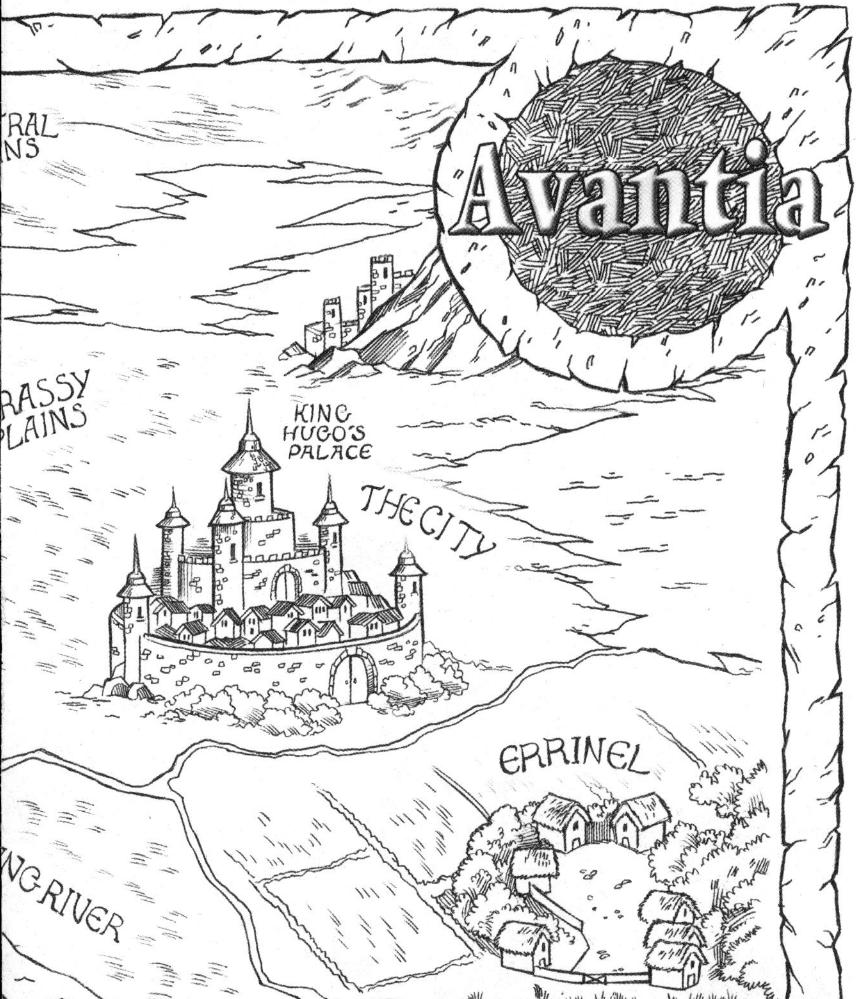

Avantia

TRAL
NS

RASSY
PLAINS

KING
HUGO'S
PALACE

THE CITY

ERRINEL

NG RIVER

L

THE DARK JUNGLE

Tremble, warriors of Avantia, for a new enemy stalks your land!

I am Sanpao, the Pirate King of Makai! My ship brings me to your shores to claim an ancient magic more powerful than any you've encountered before. No one can stand in my way, especially not that pathetic boy, Tom, or his friends. Even Aduro cannot help you this time. My pirate band will pillage and burn without mercy, and my Beasts will be more than a match for any hero in Avantia.

Pirates! Batten down the hatches and raise the sails. We come to conquer and destroy!

Sanpao, the Pirate King

PROLOGUE

"Pull!"

Abel sat on a wooden seat at the front of the caravan, urging the harnessed moose onwards across the Icy Plains. The creature snorted its wide nostrils and dug in its hooves, hauling the wooden caravan through the endless snow.

"Yes! Work! That's the way."

Abel glanced at his father, who was riding alongside the caravan. He sat on a mighty moose with antlers that spread like the branches of a tree. Abel guided the caravan over a treacherous patch of ice, his father nodding with approval at his skill.

Ahead of them, the line of creaking and groaning caravans stretched away in a dark, winding column through the snow. The tribe was seeking to trade its furs and skins for enough dried and smoked food to see it through the severe winter, when hunting became impossible.

Abel's father stared back the way they had come, and a frown passed over his weathered face.

"What is it, father?" Abel asked.

"A blizzard's coming," he growled.

A fist of unease clenched in the pit of Abel's stomach. He stood up and stared over the caravan. Behind them, the sky was a menacing swirl of grey and white.

His father dug his heels into the moose's flanks and it cantered up the column of caravans. "Make haste!" he called. "We must seek shelter!"

People turned to look, their faces grim as they saw the approaching blizzard.

Abel sat down, gripping the reins and flicking them. "Faster!" he called.

His moose lifted its head and let out a frightened bellow. Other nearby moose were tossing their antlers, eyes rolling, their hooves stamping.

They've been through blizzards before, Abel thought anxiously. *It's as if they sense something else is coming... something worse...*

A scream of terror almost stopped his heart. He turned, crying out in horror as he saw an enormous bird swooping out of the sky, wings spread, claws stretched, head thrust forwards on a long neck. It was black, its massive body dark and shining as though the feathers were coated with oil.

It was more hideous than any scavenger bird he had ever seen. And huge! The creature's head was bald, save for tufts of white feathers behind its blazing eyes. As it swooped down, enormous claws raked across the top of a caravan, tipping it onto its side and throwing the passengers into the snow with cries and screams.

Abel leaped from his moving caravan, landing in the snow and running to help the people who had been hurt. He saw the bird come down on the overturned caravan, its talons crushing the wooden

panels, its head jerking downwards,
tearing at the canvas awning.

The other moose scattered,
dragging the caravans behind them.
Goods and people fell into the snow.
Frightened voices cried out. The bird

rose on its sweeping wings and a dreadful stench wafted to Abel on the rushing winds of the coming blizzard.

The bird swooped again, snapping up a fleeing man in its beak. It shook him and tossed him into the air. Screaming, the man plunged down and lay unmoving in the snow.

The bird let out a heart-stopping cry and turned towards Abel, fixing him with its evil eyes. It rose, almost blotting out the seething sky as it hung in the air above him.

"Abel!" He was snapped out of his horrified trance by his father's urgent cry. "Go, boy. Save yourself!"

He had never heard such dread in his father's voice, and he obeyed.

He ran, the deep snow dragging at his feet. Anguish filled his heart at the thought of leaving his father behind. He did not know where he was heading. He just needed to get away from the dreadful bird.

He felt the stinking wind strike his back as the bird hovered over him. He heard its skull-shredding cries. He fell, tripping in the snow, but he was on his feet again in an instant. He half-turned towards the bird, his arms raised to try to protect himself. At that moment, with a swirl of snow, the blizzard hit, the ferocious winds sweeping around Abel and almost knocking him down.

The bird's eyes glowed, burning with a fierce red fire. Beams of blinding light burst from them.

The twin beams blasted into Abel's face, filling his vision with scorching pain. Abel clutched at his eyes and collapsed, writhing in the snow.

CHAPTER ONE

FROZEN DEATH

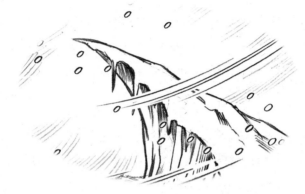

Tom reined Storm to a halt and stared out over the frozen landscape. Elenna rode up to his side on her white mare, Blizzard, given to her by a horse whisperer after their battle against the evil Beast, Koron. The breath of the two horses hung like fog in the air. Blizzard tossed her mane, snorting and stamping, as though she didn't like the look of what lay in front of them. Elenna shivered, peering ahead.

They had reached the edge of Avantia's Icy Plains.

Tom's breath gusted in white clouds as he leaned forwards and patted Storm's neck. "The temperature's dropping fast," he said.

"Will the Tree still show itself on the map after what happened last time?" Elenna asked.

Tom frowned. He knew why she was anxious. He and Elenna had sworn to protect the mystical Tree of Being from the Pirate King Sanpao and his evil crew.

The Pirate King was tracking the Tree of Being – and Sanpao had six ferocious Beasts at his command. He controlled the Beasts by using the main mast of his ship, which was cut from the magical Tree of Being.

Tom and Elenna had managed to defeat four of these Beasts so far, but Tom was in no doubt that the wicked pirate would call up another deadly foe when their paths crossed again. The Tree had mystical powers that could open portals into other worlds. The pirates wanted to use these portals to pillage and loot. *But I need the Tree for something much more important,* Tom thought. Only through its portals could they hope to rescue Elenna's wolf, Silver, and Tom's trapped mother, Freya. Both of them had been left behind in the land of Tavania, after their last Quest was completed.

But the Tree wasn't easy to find. It appeared and disappeared across the landscapes of Avantia, shooting up out of the ground for a time and then sliding back into the earth without warning. It had been very sickly and weak when Tom and Elenna had first seen it, but it had grown gradually stronger as their Quest continued.

Tom shivered again at the memory of the Tree's last disappearance. Instead of sinking into the ground, it had vanished with a crack of green lightning.

Was the Tree destroyed? Tom wondered. There was only one way to find out. Tom reached into his saddlebag and drew out the map made from the Tree's precious bark.

"If the Tree still exists, the map will show us," Tom said.

Before Tom could unroll it, a gust of icy air came whipping across the Icy Plains. He narrowed his eyes as it

snapped their clothes and clawed at
their faces and limbs. The two horses
braced themselves, their heads down,
their manes and tails flying.

"Take the map," Tom called against
the howl of the wind. He handed it
to Elenna, lifting his shield as a buffer
to shelter behind.

They huddled together as the wind whipped past them. Six tokens were embedded on the outer face of the shield. One of them was a bell from Nanook the Snow Monster, a Good Beast they had met on their very first Quest. The bell would protect them from the worst of the cold.

Elenna unrolled the map and Tom leaned in closer. Its inner skin was etched with fine lines that followed the contours of the landscape that surrounded them. The Icy Plains were clearly visible, and at the centre they saw the faint outline of the Tree of Being.

"The Tree is there!" gasped Elenna.

"But it's very pale," Tom pointed out.

"It's getting clearer," said Elenna as the lines darkened.

The Tree has survived, thought Tom,

grinning. *We can still rescue Silver and my mother.*

"The tree is just above Nanook's cave," he said. "Perhaps we'll see her again."

"I hope so," said Elenna.

"We should move quickly," said Tom. "Sanpao will be heading towards the Tree, too."

Fighting the vicious wind, Tom and Elenna rode into the Icy Plains. The frosty grass soon disappeared under a thick blanket of snow. Fresh white drifts lay all around them. The sky was heavy with iron-grey clouds, threatening more snowfall.

"I wish we had some thicker clothes," Elenna groaned, drawing her cloak closer around her shoulders.

Storm and Blizzard lifted their hooves high as they picked their way

through the drifts, but when they
came to a place where the snow was
even deeper, Tom could see that the
two horses were struggling.

"We have to dismount," he said. "Storm and Blizzard will find the going easier without our weight on them."

He jumped down into the snow, sinking to his shins. The drifts were light and powdery, and crunched under his feet. Elenna dropped from the saddle, keeping hold of Blizzard's reins as she plodded along at Tom's side.

They struggled on. Tom's boots were soaked through and the cold numbed his feet as he turned to see how Storm was faring. The gallant horse's muzzle was coated with ice crystals. Tom reached up to brush the ice away, but as he did so, his foot came up against something and he fell headlong with a cry.

"Tom! Are you alright?" Elenna

called, helping him up.

"I'm fine," he gasped, stooping and clearing the snow away with both hands. "I tripped on something."

Elenna knelt at his side and together they used their hands to scoop the snow away. They dug deeper, their hands becoming numb, their arms straining with the effort. They revealed a brown hump.

"Is it a rock?" Elenna asked.

"I think it's an animal!" said Tom, seeing a brown pelt.

They worked faster to clear the snow.

Tom could see fur, each hair frozen stiff. Heavy branching antlers. Glassy eyes staring lifelessly.

"It's a moose!" Tom exclaimed. He saw a leather harness strapped to the body of the dead creature. "This was a working animal," he said with sudden urgency. "Quickly! We need to find whatever it was harnessed to – there might be people still alive!"

CHAPTER TWO

BURIED ALIVE

They threw themselves onto their
knees and began to scoop more snow
away. Tom hacked at the snow with
his shield, throwing it over his
shoulder as he delved. At his side,
Elenna was digging with her bare
hands, her knuckles skinned and raw.

"I've found something!" she said.
Tom turned to her. It was a curve of
shaped wood.

They scraped around the object until Tom made out the spokes of a large wheel.

"A wagon," breathed Elenna.

Tom heard a muffled sound from beneath the snow.

"Someone's alive down there," he gasped.

Working frantically, they exposed part of the axle and some wooden slats. The horses backed away, whinnying anxiously as the two companions uncovered more.

It was a caravan, turned onto its side. There were intricate carvings in the wood, showing hunting scenes and people riding moose over fields of snow. At the rear of the caravan was a pair of wooden doors, thickly coated with ice.

Tom drew his sword. Grasping it in

both hands, he struck the base of the hilt against the ice. It shattered into a thousand sharp fragments.

"We should be able to get the doors open if we both push," he said.

Standing side-by-side, Tom and Elenna pressed their shoulders to the doors. They dug their heels in, using all their strength. With a creak and a crack the two small doors swung open.

The contents of the caravan were strewn and heaped about. Something moved under a pile of furs and skins. They heaved upwards and the frightened face of a boy, about their own age, appeared.

"It's all right," Elenna said. "You're safe now!"

"Thank you," he gasped, scrambling forwards. "Have you found any other survivors?"

"There's no one else here," Tom told him gently. "I'm Tom, and my friend is Elenna. We stumbled over you by accident. Your caravan was completely buried."

"My name's Abel," groaned the boy, putting his hands to his face. "The others...they must have died in the attack."

"What attacked you?" asked Tom.

The boy shuddered. "It came from the sky."

Tom looked sharply at him. "Was it a flying pirate ship?" he asked. Sanpao and his evil crew travelled in a great flying ship with blood-red sails. *Had they been here?* Tom thought.

Abel frowned in confusion. "No, it was a huge bird. It smashed into the caravans and caught people up in its claws. It was terrible!"

Tom and Elenna glanced at one another. Was this the next of the Pirate King's Beasts?

"But the worst thing about it were its eyes," Abel continued. "They were burning red. It stared at me and everything went dark." He hung his head. "I could hear people screaming. I managed to crawl into the caravan, but then the bird threw it onto its side.

I was knocked out." He took a slow breath. "When I woke up I couldn't get out."

"There's blood on your clothes," Elenna said. "Are you hurt?"

Abel lifted his shirt to reveal a long shallow wound. Tom guessed that it had been caused by the Beast's talon.

"I'll look for something to bind it," Elenna said, crawling into the caravan. Tom picked up a fur and threw it around Abel's shoulders. The boy stared blankly past Tom; Abel's eyes did not focus on him.

He was blind!

"Did the bird do that to your eyes?" Tom asked as he helped Abel out of the caravan.

Abel nodded, his face filled with misery.

"We'll do what we can to help

you," Elenna said.

They sat Abel on a pile of furs
while she took some herbs from
Storm's saddlebag and mixed them
with a handful of snow to make
a soothing poultice for his stomach
and his eyes. Elenna tore strips from
the cloth she had found in the
caravan and used them to bind
Abel's wounds.

Meanwhile, Tom went back into
the caravan, looking for something
to protect them against the cold. He
discovered blankets and thick fur
coats – as well as some dried food.

He came out with his arms full.
He placed blankets under Storm and
Blizzard's saddles. The horses snorted,
obviously glad of the warmth.

He turned to find Elenna standing
behind him. She spoke quietly. "Abel

isn't strong enough to go with us,"
she whispered. "What should we
do?"

Tom offered her a coat, and as they
both pulled on the warm furs, he
thought of a plan.

"I saw some coils of rope in the
caravan," he said. "We could attach
them to the horses' saddles and haul
the caravan upright. Then we could
harness Storm and Blizzard to it so
they can take him to the City."

Tom fetched the ropes and they tied
one end of each coil to the top of the
caravan. Then they attached the other
end to the saddles of the two horses.

"Come on, you can do it!" Tom
urged as the two horses strained on
the ropes. Gradually, creaking and
groaning, they heaved the caravan
up out of the snow. It came down on

its wheels with a thud, sending
a shower of snow tumbling from
the roof.

Elenna helped Abel into the driver's
seat while Tom harnessed the two
horses.

Tom led the horses around so that

the caravan was facing in the direction of the city. "You must go to the palace," he told Storm, stroking his muzzle. "Don't worry, we won't be parted for long."

Storm nodded his head, as though he understood what was wanted of him. Finally Tom climbed up to the driver's bench, where Elenna was tucking furs around Abel and pressing a bundle of dried food into the blind boy's hands.

"Our horses will take you to the city," he told Abel. "When you get there ask for Taladon. Tell him to be ready. Can you do that?"

Abel nodded as Elenna placed the reins of the harness in his hands.

They climbed down and Tom stood at Storm's head. "Go!" he cried, giving his faithful companion a gentle slap on the flank. Snorting, Storm and Blizzard began to pull. With a creak and rumble, the caravan moved southwards through the snow.

"Storm is wise enough to find his way home," Tom said.
"Why did you ask Abel to tell Taladon to be ready?" Elenna asked him.

"I'm afraid that Sanpao is too powerful for us to defeat on our own," Tom explained. "We may need all the help we can get." He turned towards the heart of the Icy Plains. "Now, let's find the Tree!"

CHAPTER THREE

THE CAVE OF SHADOWS

The trek northwards through the Icy Plains was slow and hard, but thankfully the thick furs kept out the worst of the bitter cold.

They plodded up a long sloping ravine that led to the lower mountain passes with bitter snow spitting into their faces. Tom and Elenna drew their furs tighter and battled up the long valley, their heads down, their eyes half-closed against the blizzard.

They came at last to a high ridge.

"I recognise this place!" Tom said. "Look. Those pine trees, and that crag. We're near Nanook's lair." He turned to Elenna. "We should ask her to help us."

"She'd be able to carry us through the snow," agreed Elenna. "We'll get to the Tree of Being much more quickly that way."

It didn't take them long to find the entrance to the cave of the Snow Monster. It lay beyond a huddle of snow-clad pine trees, halfway up a steep hillside.

They ran inside, thumping their fur cloaks to shake off the clinging snow. The great cavern was cut from a solid mass of ice, and the light that shone through the walls was bright and a little eerie. It made the cavern glitter with strange, ever-moving shadows.

"Nanook!" Tom called, running to the centre of the cavern.

His voice echoed across the lofty pinnacles of ice, but there was no sign of their old friend.

"She's probably out hunting. We should wait for her to come back," said Elenna, taking some dried meat and biscuits out of her pocket. "Let's eat while we're out of the snow."

They sat on the chilly floor and shared the food. But the flickering shadows made Tom uneasy. As he snapped a chunk from a biscuit, he noticed a shadow that seemed darker than the others, creeping across the wall. It was the shape of a tall man

with braided hair and a cutlass in
his hand.

"Sanpao!" snarled Tom. He sprang
up, drawing his sword. Elenna leapt
to her feet, fitting an arrow onto the
string of her bow.

Brandishing its cutlass at them,
the shadow danced away across the
walls towards a tunnel at the back
of the cavern.

"Quickly!" Tom cried. "Sanpao must be down that passage."

They ran after the shadow, but it flitted ahead, ducking around corners and slipping away from them.

"Turn and fight, you coward!" Tom shouted.

"What's he doing?" panted Elenna as they raced along the glowing ice tunnel. "Is he leading us into an ambush?"

At the end of the tunnel was a tall archway made out of ice blocks. Tom halted, gesturing for Elenna to do the same. He didn't want to be taken unawares by the Pirate King. Gripping his sword, he walked warily through the arch and found himself in a huge circular cavern.

Sanpao's shadow was silhouetted on the wall to Tom's right, its arms folded as though waiting for them.

Tom spun to the left, expecting to see the Pirate King standing there. "He's not here!" exclaimed Elenna. "What's going on?"

"He's using the white jewel from my belt!" Tom cried.

At the beginning of his Quest, Sanpao had placed Aduro, the Good Wizard, under his thrall. Aduro had made Tom's jewelled belt disappear, replacing it with one made from rough hide. When Tom had seen the belt again, it was around Sanpao's waist. Each jewel had magical powers, which the Pirate King was now able to use. The white jewel allowed a person's shadow to become detached and to move about on its own.

Sanpao's shadow gave them a mocking wave and vanished.

"He's gone!" Elenna breathed in relief.

"Or has he?" murmured Tom. "I think he's just playing with us for some reason. Why did he lead us here?"

A moment later, the walls of the cavern echoed as a terrifying screech sounded from beyond the archway.

Tom and Elenna spun around. The gigantic bald head of a hideous bird thrust through the entrance. Its beak stretched wide, slithers of flesh hanging from the barbed hook.

Sanpao's disembodied voice rang out on the air. "Beware Kronus the Clawed Menace!" he shouted. "You will never leave this place!"

Sanpao's trap had been sprung. The Pirate King had led them straight to the evil Beast!

CHAPTER FOUR

THE CLAWED MENACE

Kronus let out another screech as he emerged from the shadows. The Beast's vast body was coated with dark oily-looking feathers and a terrible stench wafted over them. As he swooped through the arch of ice, his huge crooked talons reached out, his horrible head swinging to and fro. Tufts of feathers jutted upwards like spikes behind his glaring eyes.

Tom and Elenna backed away, Tom moving in front of Elenna so that his shield would protect them both. He lifted his sword towards the Beast. The only way out of the ice cave was through the archway behind Kronus.

Kronus spread his monstrous wings, the feathers matted and ragged. Screeching again, he loomed over them, so that the putrid stench of his body made Tom and Elenna gag and choke. His beak snapped, his head towering above them.

"Remember what Abel said about its eyes," Tom warned Elenna. "Don't look into them."

A burning red light ignited Kronus's pupils. A moment later, two flaming red beams came shooting out from them.

Tom threw up his shield, and
the beams struck its surface with
a sizzling noise. They rebounded
and hit the wall with a searing crash.
Clouds of steam billowed up as
a great chunk of ice came crunching
down, sending frozen splinters flying.

"I'll try to shoot its eyes," cried
Elenna. She loosed an arrow, but
the Beast's head jerked aside and
the shaft glanced off the ice wall.
Enraged, Kronus sprang forwards,
his foul breath blasting them so they
were forced backwards.

Tom glanced at the archway –
moment by moment, the Beast was
driving them further from any hope
of escape.

Kronus's vicious beak stretched wide
to reveal a cavernous pink mouth and

a darting tongue. Holding his breath against the stench, Tom smashed the beak with his shield, while stabbing his sword at the Beast's body.

The Beast's head turned and the beak snapped shut on his sword blade. Tom was only just able to keep a grip on his weapon as the Beast tried to wrestle it from his grasp.

"Try again!" Tom shouted to Elenna.

But as she lined up another arrow, Kronus lashed out with a clawed foot. Tom leapt out of the way, falling into Elenna. Her arrow just missed the Beast's right eye, cutting through the tuft of quivering feathers.

Screeching with fury, Kronus backed away.

Tom slashed at the retreating Beast with his sword. With a final squawk, Kronus turned, folding his wings around his huge body, and swept through the arched entrance.

"We frightened it off!" Elenna said.

"I'm not so sure," said Tom. "Have you ever known a Beast to run away so easily? I don't think this is over."

He raced to the archway. Kronus was crouched inside the tunnel, his gaze fixed on the arch above Tom's head. Red light filled the Beast's eyes.

Tom hurled himself back into the cavern, pulling Elenna down with him, as the Beast's eyes unleashed two deadly red bolts.

He heard a crack as the beams struck the archway. Debris rained down, blocks of ice tumbling with a noise that echoed in the cavern.

As the clouds of steam evaporated, Tom saw that the archway had collapsed. Huge boulders of ice were heaped between them and the tunnel. From beyond the barrier of fallen ice, Tom heard Kronus give a final screech of triumph. Then the sound of the hideous Beast faded away.

"He's gone," Tom gasped.

"But we're trapped!" Elenna said.

Tom hacked at the ice-wall with his shield. But it wasn't soft like the snow they'd dug through on the Plains. The ice was as hard as stone. Try as he might, he could do no more than make small chips in it.

Desperation filled him. *If we can't get out, Sanpao will capture the Tree of Being and I'll never see my mother again.*

Elenna jabbed an arrow between two ice blocks, trying to lever them apart. But the arrow snapped.

An awful realisation came over Tom.

"Kronus has left us here to die!"

CHAPTER FIVE

FOOTPRINTS IN THE SNOW

"You could summon Nanook to help us," Elenna suggested, pointing to the Good Beast's bell on Tom's shield.

Tom's hand hovered over the token, but he thought about the Pirate King. How close to the Tree of Being was he now?

"We don't have time!" Tom cried. "While we're stuck in this cavern, who knows where Nanook is? In the meantime, Sanpao is hunting for the Tree. We can't let him find it before us."

Elenna glanced at his hide belt, frowning in thought. "What about the scale left by Torno when we defeated him?"

Tom's eyes lit up. "Yes! It might be able to help." He took the shiny scale from the belt and held it on the flat of his hand. Tom had received a token from each of Sanpao's defeated Beasts. Every one had magical powers, but Tom never knew what they could do until he used them in battle. And he could only use each token once – after that, they disappeared. As they stared at the scale, it began to glow.

"It's getting warmer," said Tom. "Perhaps it will melt the ice." He pressed the scale against an ice block. The ice began to hiss and steam and with surprising speed, a hole appeared. Water bubbled and flowed down as the hole widened and deepened.

Tom and Elenna gazed at one another in excitement.

"Thank goodness!" said Elenna.

Tom nodded. "We're not going to die here, after all!" he said, stepping forwards into the expanding hole and holding the scale out in front of him.

"Sanpao isn't as clever as he thinks he is!" Elenna walked behind Tom, the ice water flooding over their feet as the boulders melted away.

A few moments later they were sprinting along the winding tunnel, back into Nanook's cave. Tom felt the warmth fade from his hand. He looked down. The scale had disappeared.

"Just like the other tokens," he muttered. The gifts left by Sanpao's Beasts could only be used once, before they magically vanished.

"Should we wait for Nanook?" wondered Elenna.

Tom shook his head. "We've been delayed too long by Sanpao's traps. We have to move quickly!"

They hurried out onto the mountainside and began to scramble upwards. The map had shown them that the Tree was above Nanook's cavern. *It can't be far away now*, Tom thought.

"At least it's stopped snowing," panted Elenna between breaths.

The clouds hung low around the upper slopes of the mountain, but through the grey haze, Tom saw

a large dark shape looming above
them. He strained his eyes, trying to
work out what it was. Then he let
out a sharp breath as the clouds
parted to reveal wooden battlements
and turrets, and above them,
billowing blood-red sails.

"It's Sanpao's ship," he said. "He's
already here!"

The clouds thinned as they climbed,
and they could clearly see the ship's

flag fluttering against the pale sky, decorated with a Beast skull – the terrible symbol of the Pirate King.

A voice rang out from the ship. "Landing party ready!"

Tom and Elenna dived behind a hump of ice as the last shreds of cloud blew away from the hovering pirate ship. They watched from their hiding place as pirates threw thick ropes over the sides of the ship. The ropes coiled down to the mountainside and moments later the crew began to lower themselves over the rails.

The first man to drop into the snow shook himself and grumbled loudly. "Ach! It's cold enough to freeze your heart in your chest!"

"Should I set fire to your clothes to warm you up?" suggested another, setting the rest of the party laughing.

The evil crew gathered in the shadow of their great ship, shivering in their sleeveless jerkins, stamping their feet and rubbing their arms for warmth. Even from a distance, Tom could make out the Beast skull tattoo branded onto the forearm of each of the pirates.

Finally, Sanpao himself came sliding down a rope and landed lightly among his men. He was the tallest of them all, his scarred face twisted into a grin, his thumbs tucked into the jewelled belt that he had stolen from Tom. His hair coiled in an oiled plait studded with spikes.

As he saw the cruel expression on the Pirate King's face, Tom clenched his fists, thinking of the damage the pirates had done in Avantia.

"Our mission is almost complete!"
Sanpao shouted to his men. "The
Beast has done my bidding."
His voice took on a mocking tone.
"I know we are all deeply upset that
the two brats will perish in the cave."
The pirates howled with wicked

laughter as Sanpao continued.
"But at least it means they won't be getting in the way! The Tree of Being will be ours!"

The pirates cheered. Tom and Elenna glanced at one another.

"Sanpao's underestimated us again!" he whispered.

Sanpao raised his arms for silence. "Soon, Avantia and every other land the Tree can lead us to will be at our mercy!" he cried. "And how much mercy will we show?"

"None!" howled the pirate crew.

"Split up into search parties," roared Sanpao. "I know you're cold, my lads, but the sooner you find the Tree the sooner we can sail to warmer lands!"

Tom and Elenna watched as the pirates divided up into groups and set off in different directions.

"We'll follow Sanpao's band," Tom whispered. "Stay out of sight."

Elenna nodded and they slipped along the mountainside, keeping low and using the cover of the pine trees and the deep snow drifts as they tracked the Pirate King and his men.

The pirates trudged along a deep, snow-filled valley, Sanpao in the lead. He raised his hand. "Stop!" he demanded. "There are footprints here. A trail of huge footprints in the snow."

Tom and Elenna were crouching behind a pine tree. "It must be Nanook," Tom whispered.

Sanpao let out a spiteful laugh. "I say we warm ourselves up with a fine hunt!" he declared. "Anything that leaves such big tracks must be large enough to feed us all."

"We'll capture it and roast it alive!" shouted one of the pirates.

The others bellowed their approval. Tom's face twisted in disgust at the bloodthirsty glee of Sanpao and his crew. He turned to Elenna. "I wonder if they'll be so keen on the idea when they find their quarry is a Beast!" he murmured to her.

"Can I see the map?" Elenna whispered back. "It may help us."

Tom unrolled the map, and saw they weren't far from the Tree of Being.

"Nanook must have sensed the power of the Tree and been drawn to it," said Elenna. "She must intend to protect it."

Tom frowned. "You know what this means, don't you?" he said grimly. "Nanook is accidentally leading the pirates straight to their prize!"

CHAPTER SIX

THE SNOW MONSTER

Tom and Elenna trailed the pirate band through the snow as they followed Nanook's footprints. Tom was wet through, his hands and feet numb with cold. Elenna's teeth chattered as she ran along at his side. At last, the pirates rounded a shoulder of the mountain and Sanpao give a roar of triumph.

"We've found it, lads!"

Tom felt a surge of anxiety as he crept to the edge of the rock and peered around.

On the horizon stood the Tree of Being, looking healthier than ever. Its high branches were covered in emerald leaves and even from where he was hiding, Tom could see that it was almost restored to its full glory.

But the mighty Tree was not the only thing that took Tom's gaze. Stepping over the horizon, beating her chest with her hands, was Nanook the Snow Monster. Her eyes gleamed against her shaggy white fur and her massive yellow claws scythed the air.

She bellowed and some of the pirates drew back, but Sanpao roared with laughter, rubbing his hands together. "We should thank this Beast," he cried. "She's led us straight to the Tree." His eyes gleamed as he looked at his men. "Are we going to let this great hunk of fur hold us

back?" he shouted. "Gordok, hand me my horn!"

A man stepped forwards, giving Sanpao a long curling horn. The Pirate King put it to his lips and let out a harsh, braying blast.

From the distance, Tom and Elenna heard answering calls. "He's summoning the rest of the crew," Tom said uneasily. "Come on – we have to help Nanook protect the Tree."

Running at a low crouch, they circled the pirates, making for the high ground where Nanook stood, watching Sanpao's men. The Good Beast roared a challenge to the pirates as they drew their weapons and moved towards her.

Tom and Elenna sprinted to the cover of freezing snowdrifts, panting and chilled to the bone. Elenna suddenly skidded to a halt. "Look out!"

A great crevasse gaped in front of them like a waiting mouth, its raw stone throat plunging down. Tom couldn't stop, and leaped across, only just managing to catch hold of the far side. He scrabbled with his feet and strained his arms to haul himself up and over the lip of ice.

He waved to Elenna to show he was all right, and then beckoned for her to follow.

Elenna didn't like heights but she'd always managed to overcome this fear before. She took a few paces back, hesitated, then ran forwards and jumped. For a dreadful moment he watched her hanging in the air, her legs flailing and her eyes widening in fear as she reached out to him.

"Help me, Tom!" she cried.

He threw himself forwards and
caught hold of her wrist. It felt as
though his arm was being pulled out
of its socket by her weight. He began
to slither towards the edge.

Squirming onto his side, he managed to unsheath his sword. He dug it deep into the ice, using it to anchor him while he strained to pull Elenna to safety.

"I won't let you fall!" Tom hissed between gritted teeth.

Elenna came up over the rim of the crevasse, her face twisted with the effort, her feet kicking into the ice-wall.

A few moments later, the two friends were both lying safe on the ice, gasping for breath. They could hear the pirates shouting from beyond a snow bank.

"I'm alright, before you ask," Elenna gasped.

"Good. No time to rest," Tom panted. They clambered to their feet and ran on, using the cover of a long bank of snow to keep them from being seen.

At last they broke cover and came out into the open. Nanook turned towards them and roared a greeting, lifting her great muscular arms above her head and stamping her massive feet as though overjoyed to see her old friends.

Sanpao's band had almost reached the Good Beast, brandishing their cutlasses. Tom saw that the rest of the ship's crew was coming, swarming over the snow in answer to Sanpao's horn-blast.

He scrambled down a final deep bank of snow and came out onto a wide level expanse of ice.

The Tree has appeared in the middle of a frozen lake! he realized.

The ice was so thick under his feet

that it was almost black. He saw
Elenna's feet slither as she came to
his side.

"Take my hand!" he told her. "We
can support each other."

The pirates howled in anger as they
saw Tom and Elenna racing over the
slick ice field. Nanook growled in
welcome and turned to face their
enemies.

An angry voice boomed out over
the lake. "So, you managed to escape
the tomb Kronus made for you."
roared Sanpao. "So much the better.
Now I will be able to watch you die
with my own eyes!"

"That won't be so easy," Tom called
back. "Not with this Good Beast at
our side!"

Sanpao gave a great howl of
laughter. "Come on, my lads,"

shouted the Pirate King. "We've nothing to fear!"

"Why is he so sure of himself?" asked Elenna, fitting an arrow to her bow as the pirate hoard swarmed towards them.

"I don't know," Tom replied. He heard Nanook give a curious groan. He looked up at her. The Snow Monster was holding her huge hairy hands up to her forehead, her eyes closed tightly and her face contorted as though in pain.

"Nanook?" cried Elenna. "What's wrong?"

Anger flashed through Tom. "It's Sanpao," he snarled. "He's using the ruby jewel on my belt to communicate with Nanook. He's trying to make her obey him!"

CHAPTER SEVEN

ARROWS OF FIRE

Elenna reached up to touch Nanook's shaggy fur. "Fight it!" she urged the distressed Beast. "Don't let him take control of you!"

Nanook swayed from side to side, baring her lips in a snarl of pain, her hands pressed to either side of her head.

If Sanpao manages to control her, Tom thought, *Nanook will turn against us!*

Most of Sanpao's crew were closing in, racing across the ice, shouting and cursing. Many of them had crossbows and quivers of bolts slung over their shoulders. The Pirate King himself was at their head, his cutlass raised as he ran over the frozen lake.

"Shoot, my lads!" shouted Sanpao. "Let loose the fire-darts!"

The pirates with the crossbows raised their weapons high, and let fly with a volley of black arrows.

Tom lifted his shield as the arrows came speeding down. At first they looked like nothing more than normal arrows whittled from dark wood, but as they increased their speed, tiny flames gleamed around their shafts. As they struck the ice, they exploded in a shower of sparks that burned holes in the frozen surface. Columns of steam spiralled off into the cold air.

"What new weapon is this?" cried Elenna.

One of the arrows exploded close to Nanook, the sparks flying up and singeing her fur. She staggered away from the heat, roaring in anger. Tom knew that as a Beast who lived in the frozen wilderness, these weapons would terrify her.

Another arrow sped towards Nanook. Tom jumped up and deflected it away from her with his shield. The shaft skidded across the ice, failing to ignite. It lay smoking and sizzling with heat. Elenna ran to fetch it, swiftly fitting it to her bow and shooting it back at the pirates. The arrow exploded just ahead of their enemies, sending sparks flying

and knocking two of Sanpao's men
off their feet.

"Well done!" Tom shouted to
Elenna.

During the attack with the burning
arrows, Sanpao and the rest of his
crew had held back, but now they
came charging across the ice,
bellowing and slashing the air with
their cutlasses.

Tom gripped his sword and broke
into a run, heading straight for the
Pirate King.

*If I can defeat Sanpao, the rest of his
crew might turn tail and run!*

Sanpao's cruel eyes gleamed with
pleasure.

"Cutlass against sword!" he shouted.
"Let's see which is the mightier!" He
bounded forwards, whirling the

curved blade about his head.

Tom sprang at him, his shield on his arm, his sword gleaming as he brought it down to clash with bone-jarring force against Sanpao's flashing blade. The blow drove down Sanpao's arm so the point of his weapon scored a deep groove in the ice.

But Sanpao bounded to one side, slicing up with his cutlass, managing to twist his blade past Tom's shield.

Tom hurled himself back, but he felt a sudden sharp pain at the side of his jaw. The tip of the cutlass had cut him! He took several steps back, bringing his hand up to his chin. There was warm blood on his fingers, but the wound didn't seem deep.

I'll have to be more careful, he thought.

"First blood to me!" roared Sanpao.

"Come on, boy. I'm not done with you yet. I'll take your head from your shoulders next time and use it as a figurehead on my ship!"

"Not while there's blood in my veins," shouted Tom.

"Then I'll empty those veins of yours!" Sanpao bragged. "And I'll drink your blood from a golden cup."

Tom ran forwards again, but he saw a second flight of black arrows curving through the air. They soared in a hissing arc over his head and he swung round. The arrows crashed into the ice next to Elenna and Nanook, sending up showers of sparks and splinters of ice. Elenna was jumping from side to side to avoid the teeming arrows, shooting her own bow at every opportunity. Nanook stood in front of the Tree of

Being, bellowing and warding the arrows away from the Tree with her great arms.

"You don't seem to like my burning arrows," Sanpao mocked. "I thought you would welcome some warmth in this frozen waste!"

Spurred on by Sanpao's taunts, Tom launched himself at the Pirate King. But Sanpao sprang backwards, flipping head over heels, his cutlass scything the air. He landed in a crouch, his face twisted into a cruel smirk.

"I'll fight you to the death, boy!" Sanpao roared. "But before I finish you off, you'll see your friend killed in front of your eyes!" He laughed, pointing upwards with his cutlass.

A wide dark shadow swooped over the ice lake and a terrible screech ripped across the sky. Tom looked up.

Kronus was speeding down, his ragged black wings spread, his claws reaching and his hooked beak wide open. He was heading straight for Elenna.

CHAPTER EIGHT

BATTLE OF THE BEASTS

"Elenna! Watch out!" Tom shouted.

She whipped around at the sound of his voice. As the Beast dove at her, she threw herself to the ground, rolling out of reach. Kronus's talons raked the ice a hair's breadth from her, and the Beast screeched in frustration as he missed his prey.

Elenna jumped to her feet, fitting an arrow to her bow and shooting.

As Kronus wheeled around to attack again, the arrow pierced the tip of his right wing. Shrieking in pain, the Beast beat his great wings, rising into the air, twisting his head on its long neck and biting at the arrow.

Tom spun around, expecting the Pirate King to be right behind him. But Sanpao had moved away and

was standing close to the Tree of Being. He was gesturing to his men and pointing his cutlass at the great trunk. "Axemen," he shouted to them. "Cut the Tree down!"

Two pirates carrying huge bone-handled axes swarmed towards the Tree of Being, leaving the others to continue the fight with Tom and Elenna and Nanook.

The Good Beast stood braced in front of the Tree, her long arms swinging like scythes, sending men spinning through the air as they attacked. But Tom saw that pirates with axes were running around her, trying to reach the Tree from behind.

I must help! Tom thought.

He sprinted towards the Good Beast, but a fearsome shadow swept darkly over the ice and a familiar, overpowering stench filled the air.

Kronus had returned to the fight!

The hideous Beast plummeted down, screeching and snapping his beak, his talons reaching out. Nanook lifted her head, bellowing in rage as she caught sight of the dreadful bird. She threw up her arms to snatch the Beast out of the air.

Kronus hung above Nanook's head, beating the air with his oily-black wings. She lunged and sank her talons into Nanook's forearms, digging deep into the Good Beast's white fur so that drops of blood splashed down onto the ice.

"Nanook!" Tom cried, horrified by the sight of the Good Beast's wounds.

The pirates drew back from the warring Beasts, watching the mighty battle from a safe distance. The Good

Beast howled in pain as she struggled against Kronus's crushing grip. Kronus's wings flapped like a ragged black cloak and his long neck writhed as he tried to peck at Nanook's face. The roaring of the two battling Beasts made the ice shake under Tom's feet.

"I'm coming, Nanook!" Tom shouted. As he ran towards her, a pirate stepped into his path, raising his cutlass. Tom lashed out with his shield, catching the pirate under the chin and lifting him off his feet. With a groan, the pirate went skidding away across the ice.

Nanook threw herself from side to side, desperately trying to free her arms from Kronus' vicious grip. But the evil Beast hovered over her as he tried to force Nanook to look into his raging red eyes.

The red beams will blind her! Tom thought. *She'll be helpless!*

"Nanook! Avoid his eyes!" Elenna shouted, giving voice to Tom's fears.

But Nanook ripped one arm free of the claws and her great hand snatched Kronus's throat. Shrieking, the evil Beast pulled out of her grip, his beak stabbing at Nanook's face.

Nanook leapt up with a roar, grabbing Kronus's body. But she fell back with only oily feathers clutched in both hands. Tom reached the Tree, under the shadow of Kronus's huge flailing wings, and his nostrils were filled with the dreadful bird's stench.

Tom had to jump aside to avoid being trampled by Nanook's feet. Blood sprayed from her wounds, but Tom could see that she was twisting Kronus's head on its neck, wrenching it upwards so the eye beams were directed into the sky.

The flying Beast thrashed his wings more ferociously, writhing in Nanook's grip as he fought desperately to get free. The weight

of the struggling Beast was too much
for Nanook to control. Tom saw her
feet slither on the ice, and her massive
shadow fell over him as she toppled.
Tom flung himself out of the way.

Roaring and screaming, the Beasts
crashed down onto the ice together,
landing in the spot where Tom had

been. The impact sent tremors across the ice. Elenna managed to keep her balance, but many of the pirates fell to their knees.

Tom stood up. The ice rocked and trembled under him and he heard loud snapping sounds. Like the threads of a spider's web, cracks fanned out over the lake from where the two Beasts battled.

Tom spread his arms, widening his stance as he fought for balance on the tipping ice floe. He heard a boom and saw the Tree of Being's branches quivering. Then it lurched to one side, toppling slowly as it began to sink into the lake.

At least Sanpao won't get the Tree this time! Tom thought as the trembling branches began to disappear under the icy, churning water.

CHAPTER NINE

THE ICE LAKE

The pirates roared with anger as the Tree of Being shook in the breaking ice. Already, half its length was under the foaming water – but Sanpao ran forwards, bellowing in rage and swinging an axe.

Tom jumped into his path, determined to keep the Pirate King at bay until the Tree had vanished.

I may not be able to use the Tree to save

my mother, he thought as Sanpao bore down on him, *but I'll keep it out of their clutches!*

A ferocious roar from Nanook drew Tom's attention away from the pirates for a moment. The Good Beast stood upright again, both her powerful hands gripped around Kronus' neck. Her face twisted by the effort, Nanook dashed the bird to the ice. More cracks fanned out and clear lake water spurted and gushed up between the ice blocks.

But even as he writhed and shrieked on the ice, Kronus caught Nanook with his clawed talons, pulling her down again. Suddenly, the ice sheet that Tom was standing on broke away, and lurched on the churning water. Spray fountained up between him and Sanpao. Tom

crouched low, planting his legs firmly,
stretching his arms out for balance.
From the corner of his eye, he saw
Nanook lash out with a fist, catching

the evil Beast on the side of his head, snapping it sideways on the long, scraggy neck. Screeching in agony, Kronus broke away and rose into the air, shaking his head. He fired beams of red light from his eyes, which cut across the ice, breaking the floes and sending pillars of steam gushing into the air.

Why isn't he aiming at Nanook? Tom wondered.

Kronus screeched, his head jerking downwards, his neck elongating. He seemed to have spotted something that made him furious. But there was nothing there, save the dazzling white ice – on which was a perfect image of Kronus.

He's attacking his own reflection, Tom realised. *That blow from Nanook must have confused him.*

"You'll never get to the Tree!" he heard Elenna shout. He spun around in time to see her using the end of her quiver to send a pirate toppling into the freezing water. The pirate floundered in the foam, snatching hold of the ice floe over which Kronus was hovering. The

ice sheet tipped under the pirate's weight, the Beast's reflection vanished. Screaming, Kronus veered away and went hurtling up high into the sky.

As the Tree of Being sank, the suction made the water swirl, pushing the ice floes away from each other. Tom leapt across the widening stretch of water between him and Elenna. He could see Sanpao racing across the ice, jumping from one sheet to another and heading for the Tree.

"Cut it down!" he shouted to his scattered crew. "Before it's too late!"

With a final bound, Sanpao reached the lurching tree. Snatching an axe from his belt he raised it high, aiming for the tree trunk.

I need to get closer! Tom realised. He turned to Elenna.

"Spin me!" he cried, reaching out his hand. Understanding what was

needed, Elenna grasped his hand in both of hers and turned on her heels. Tom spun in a circle around her, his knees flexed, his sword ready.

"Now!" he shouted. Elenna released him and he went skidding over the ice towards the Pirate King. His momentum carried him over the gaps between the parted blocks. He leant left and right to skim past the pirates in his path, ducking down to avoid swinging cutlasses, dodging away from grasping arms. Before Sanpao had time to jump aside, Tom struck him with the full force of his shield.

The Pirate King sprawled onto the ice, the axe skimming out of his grip. Snarling in anger, Sanpao climbed to his knees, when the ice shook again and the air was filled with a sucking, gurgling noise.

"The Tree!" shouted Elenna. Tom turned to see the great Tree of Being disappearing under the churning water. With a final roar and an eruption of foam, the upper branches slipped away. *Just like before!*

"Close, but not close enough, Sanpao!" he shouted. The Tree had disappeared into the water, just as it had disappeared below the ground before. Tom was certain that they would find it again.

Shaking with fury, Sanpao howled orders at his men. "Get back to the ship! We need to chart a course for the next place the Tree will appear!"

The pirates turned, flooding away over the splitting ice floes. Bellowing, Nanook pursued them, swiping at them with her claws, beating them with her fists as they fled in disarray.

Sanpao turned to Tom, an evil grin on his face. "I fear it's a final goodbye this time," he said as Elenna arrived at Tom's side. "But don't be too sad at our parting. I'm not leaving you entirely alone!" He pointed to the sky, then turned and went racing across the ice.

Tom looked up.

Hovering above them on vast black wings was Kronus, his eyes burning like furnace fires as he prepared to unleash his deadly beams.

CHAPTER TEN

STOWAWAYS

Tom lifted his sword high. "Come on, Kronus! Come and get me!"

The Beast screeched and tipped into a dive.

Tom glanced at Elenna. "Run," he told her. "I'll be right behind you. I know what I'm doing."

Elenna gave him a doubtful look, but she nodded and ran to the edge of the floe, leaping onto another.

Tom watched as the Beast plunged towards him. The fire grew in Kronus's red eyes.

He prepared himself, flexing his legs, his muscles tensing.

Any…moment…now!

At the same instant that the red beams came shooting downwards, Tom leapt aside.

Kronus stared at his own hurtling mirror image. He screeched at the

reflected bird and shot down twin beams with a rush and a hiss. The floe burst into fragments and the great Beast plummeted into the icy lake. Steam gushed up as the waters crashed and foamed.

Tom and Elenna grasped one another as the floe they were on tipped violently in the swell. But then the turmoil of the water subsided and everything became still.

The Beast had gone.

Tom stepped to the edge of the floe. Something was bobbing on the surface. He reached out with his sword, guiding it towards him then crouched to fish it out. It was a glassy globe, glowing blue and red, just large enough to sit comfortably on his palm. The Beast's eye. He stood up, showing it to Elenna.

"The next token," she said. "I wonder what it does."

"We'll find out in good time," said Tom, slipping the cool orb into his tunic. "Let's get off this lake before the ice breaks up even more."

Moving cautiously, and helping one another over gaps in the ice, they made their way to the edge of the lake. Nanook was waiting for them there, grunting in a satisfied way as she watched the pirates fleeing over the snow.

Tom took out the map. "We can't let the pirates get ahead of us again," he said. Nanook stood over them like a shaggy white haystack.

"The Tree's already reappeared," said Elenna, pointing at the map.

"And it's in the city this time," said Tom grimly. "How are we going to get there before the pirates? We have no horses and they have their flying ship."

"Could Nanook take us?" Elenna suggested.

"We can't ask her to leave the Icy Plains," Tom pointed out.

Before anything more could be said, the air ahead of them shimmered. A faint voice drifted towards them; it was Aduro.

"My strength is returning slowly," the Good Wizard said. "Sanpao's spell is wearing off. I cannot make myself visible to you yet, but I can give you these words of advice: look to the skies!" And then the voice was gone and the shimmering faded from the air.

Puzzled, Tom looked up. A heap of garments was falling towards them. They stepped back as the things came down with a soft thump.

"Pirate bandanas," exclaimed Elenna, picking up one of the headbands. It had the tell-tale Beast skull on it. "And pirate jerkins."

"I know what Aduro wants us to do!" said Tom. "We should disguise ourselves and hide on board Sanpao's ship. That way he'll take us to the city without even knowing it."

"And Nanook can carry us to the ship," suggested Elenna. "If she runs, we'll easily get there ahead of the pirates."

They quickly grabbed up the bandannas and jerkins and put them on. Tom pointed to himself and Elenna and then to Nanook's arms, turning and pointing out across the snowy landscape.

Grunting her understanding, the Snow Monster picked them up and began to run, her feet pounding through the deep snow. She raced down a long curved valley, avoiding the path taken by the fleeing pirates. They crossed a ridge and saw Sanpao's ship ahead. It floated above the mountainside where the pirates had left it, but the decks looked quiet.

"We beat them!" smiled Elenna,

as they reached the vessel.

Nanook crept up beneath the ship
and lifted them so that they were
able to climb the ropes dangling over
the side. They heaved themselves
over the rail.

"Thanks, old friend," Tom called
down to the Good Beast. "You'd
better hide now."

Nanook strode away, turning once to raise an arm in farewell. Soon she was invisible in the endless snow.

The deck was covered in barrels and coils of rope, its timbers rotting in places. The tall mast, with the sails tied, loomed over them. At the aft, a raised platform stood over the deck.

"We should hide," said Tom. "Before..."

He heard the voices of the pirates below. They sounded angry and quarrelsome.

"Get aboard!" Sanpao shouted. "We've no time to lose."

As the pirates swarmed up the ropes, Tom and Elenna flung themselves behind the great wheel. They found a box filled with cutlasses, and they took one each. They watched between the wheel spokes as the deck filled with the ruffian crew. Sanpao was the last to come onboard. He stood on the platform, his cutlass raised.

"Set sail, my lads!" he roared. "We're heading for our final victory!"

"To victory!" shouted the men, brandishing their cutlasses. "To the Pirate King!"

Tom and Elenna slipped from cover and mingled with the pirates, lifting their cutlasses and joining in the chant.

But Tom had a different toast in mind. He turned to Elenna. "To Avantia!" he murmured under his breath. "And to the downfall of Sanpao!"

As the pirates cheered and slashed the air with their cutlasses, the ropes were drawn up and the great ship

lifted into the sky. A breath of wind
caught in the blood red sails and
the ship skimmed the mountains,
heading for the distant city and the
next stage of the Quest.

"I wonder if Abel will get to the city
before us," whispered Elenna. He
should have taken a message to
Taladon and Aduro to prepare.

"I hope so," Tom replied. "With my
father at our side, we'll sink Sanpao
once and for all."

Join Tom on the last stage
of the Beast Quest when he will face

BLOODBOAR
THE BURIED
DOOM

Win an exclusive
Beast Quest T-shirt and goody bag!

Tom has battled many fearsome Beasts and we want to know which one is your favourite! Send us a drawing or painting of your favourite Beast and tell us in 30 words why you think it's the best.

Each month we will select **three** winners to receive a Beast Quest T-shirt and goody bag!

Send your entry on a postcard to
BEAST QUEST COMPETITION
Orchard Books, 338 Euston Road, London NW1 3BH.

Australian readers should email:
childrens.books@hachette.com.au

New Zealand readers should write to:
Beast Quest Competition, 4 Whetu Place, Mairangi Bay, Auckland NZ, or email: childrensbooks@hachette.co.nz

**Don't forget to include your name and address.
Only one entry per child.**

Good luck!

Join the Quest,
Join the Tribe

www.beastquest.co.uk

Have you checked out the Beast Quest website?
It's the place to go for games, downloads, activities,
sneak previews and lots of fun!

You can read all about your favourite Beasts, down-
load free screensavers and desktop wallpapers for
your computer, and even challenge your friends
to a Beast Tournament.

Sign up to the newsletter at www.beastquest.co.uk
to receive exclusive extra content and the opportunity to enter special members-only competitions.
We'll send you up-to-date info on all the Beast
Quest books, including the next exciting series
which features six brand-new Beasts!

Get 30% off all Beast Quest Books at www.beastquest.co.uk
Enter the code BEAST at the checkout.

All books priced at £4.99,
special bumper editions
priced at £5.99.

Orchard Books are available from all good bookshops, or can
be ordered from our website: www.orchardbooks.co.uk,
or telephone 01235 827702, or fax 01235 8227703.

Series 8: THE PIRATE KING
COLLECT THEM ALL!

Sanpao the Pirate King wants to steal the sacred Tree of Being. Can Tom scupper his plans?

978 1 40831 310 7

KORON
JAWS OF DEATH

978 1 40831 311 4

HECTON
THE BODY SNATCHER

978 1 40831 312 1

TORNO
THE HURRICANE DRAGON

978 1 40831 313 8

KRONUS
THE CLAWED MENACE

978 1 40831 314 5

BLOODBOAR
THE BURIED DOOM

978 1 40831 315 2

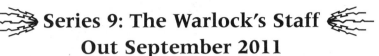 **Series 9: The Warlock's Staff**
Out September 2011

Meet six terrifying new Beasts!

Ursus the Clawed Roar
Minos the Demon Bull
Koraka the Winged Assassin
Silver the Wild Terror
Spikefin the Water King
Torpix the Twisting Serpent

 **Watch out for the next
Special Bumper
Edition
OUT OCT 2011!**

FROM THE DARK, A HERO ARISES...

Dare to enter the kingdom of Avantia.

A new evil arises in Avantia. Lord Derthsin has ordered his armies into the four corners of Avantia. If the four Beasts of Avantia can find their Chosen Riders they might have the strength to challenge Derthsin. But if they fail, the land of Avantia will be lost forever...

FIRST HERO, CHASING EVIL AND CALL TO WAR, OUT NOW!

Fire and Fury out July 2011

www.chroniclesofavantia.com